beast feast

For my son Raphaël

ISBN 0-590-99488-3

Copyright © 1994 by Douglas Florian.
All rights reserved.
Published by Scholastic Inc., 555 Broadway, New York, NY 10012,
by arrangement with Harcourt Brace & Co., Inc.
TRUMPET and the TRUMPET logo
are registered trademarks of Scholastic Inc.

12 11 10 9 8 7 6 5 4 3 2   1/0

Printed in the U.S.A.

The paintings in this book were done in watercolor
on cold-press French watercolor paper.
The display type was set in Pabst and
the text type was set in Sabon.
Designed by Lisa Peters.

Contents

The Walrus

The pounding spatter
Of salty sea
Makes the walrus
Walrusty.

8

The Barracuda

In all the world
Nothing's ruder
Than a hungry
Barracuda.

The Anteater

The
    anteater's
        long
           and
               tacky
                   tongue
                      is
                         snaking
                             from
                                 its
                             snout.

A thousand termites riding in,
But no one riding out.

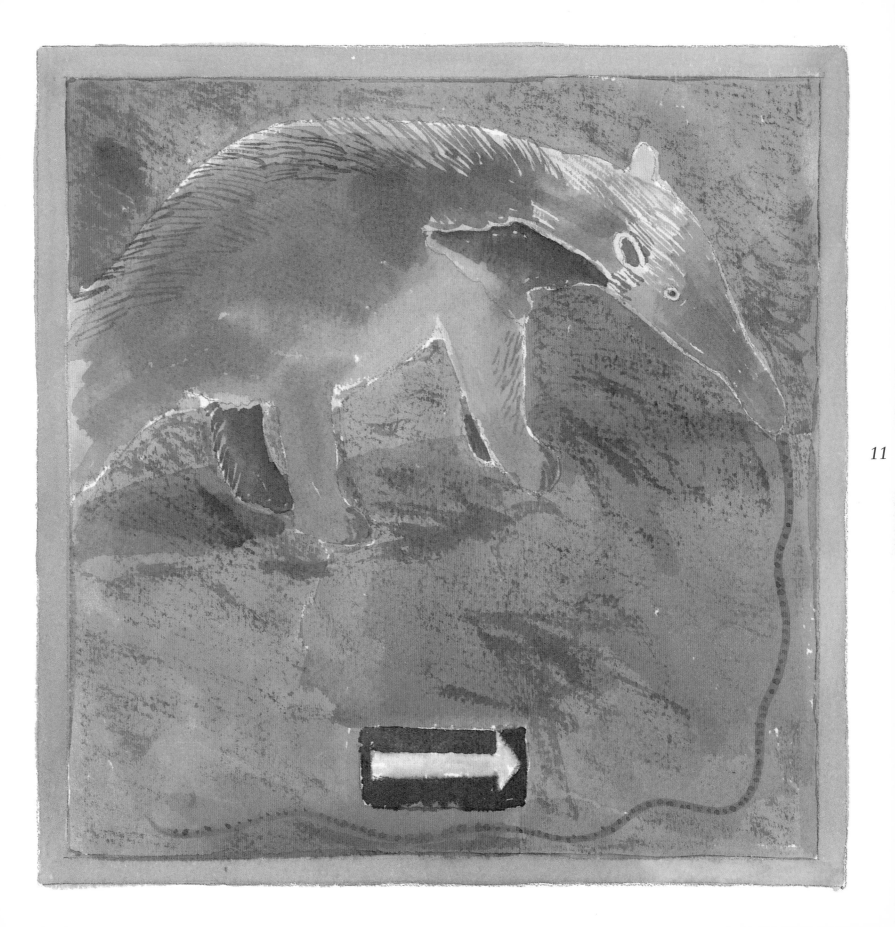

The Boa

Just when you think you know the boa,
There's moa and moa and moa and moa.

The Lobster

See the hard-shelled
Leggy lobster
Like an underwater
Mobster
With two claws
To catch and crush
Worms and mollusks
Into mush
And antennae
Long and thick
Used for striking
Like a stick.
So be careful
On vacation
Not to step on
This crustacean.

The Chameleon

Although it may seem very strange,
The colors on a chameleon change
From mousy browns to leafy greens
And several colors in between.
Its very long and sticky tongue
On unsuspecting bugs is sprung.
It lashes out at rapid rates
On unaware invertebrates,
Then just as quickly will retract
With flabbergasted fly intact.
So bugs beware this risky reptilian —
The clever everchanging chameleon.

The Rhea

The rhea rheally isn't strange —
It's just an ostrich, rhearranged.

The Ants

Ants are scantily
Half an inch long,
But for their size
They're very strong.
Ants tote leaves
Fives times their weight
Back to their nest
At speedy rate.
They walk on tree limbs
Upside down
A hundred feet
Above the ground,
While down below
Beneath a mound
They're building tunnels
Underground.
And so it's been —
And it will be —
Since greatest
Ant antiquity.

The Whale

Big as a street —
With fins, not feet —
I'm full of blubber,
With skin like rubber.
When I breathe out,
I s p e w   a spout.
I swim by the shore
And eat more and more.
I'm very, very hard to ignore.

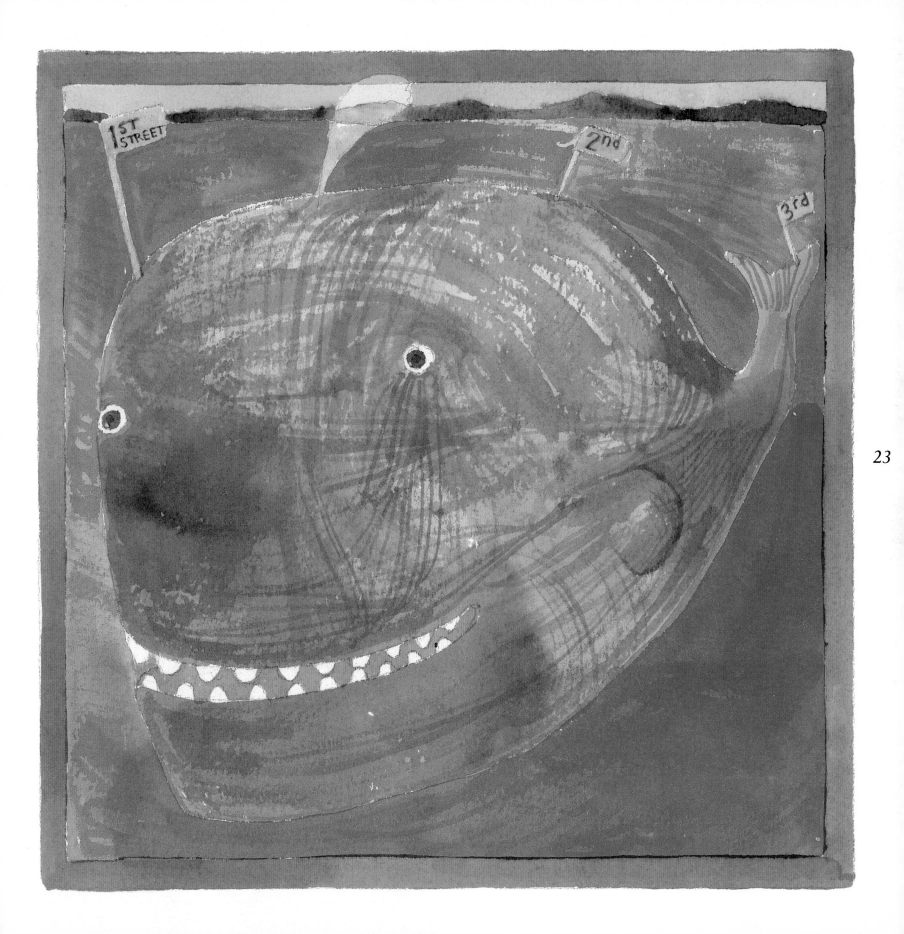

23

24

The Pigeon

I don't claim to
Love the pigeon,
But I like it
Just a smidgen.
Pigeons don't get
No respect
Just because they
Hunt and peck.
When they walk
Their heads go bobbin' —
You don't see that
In a robin.
They will sit right
On your shoulder.
Not too many
Birds are bolder.
Just be thankful
They're around
To pick up crumbs
Left on the ground.

The Armadillo

The armadillo
As a pillow
Would really be swell
Except
For the fact
That it comes in a shell.

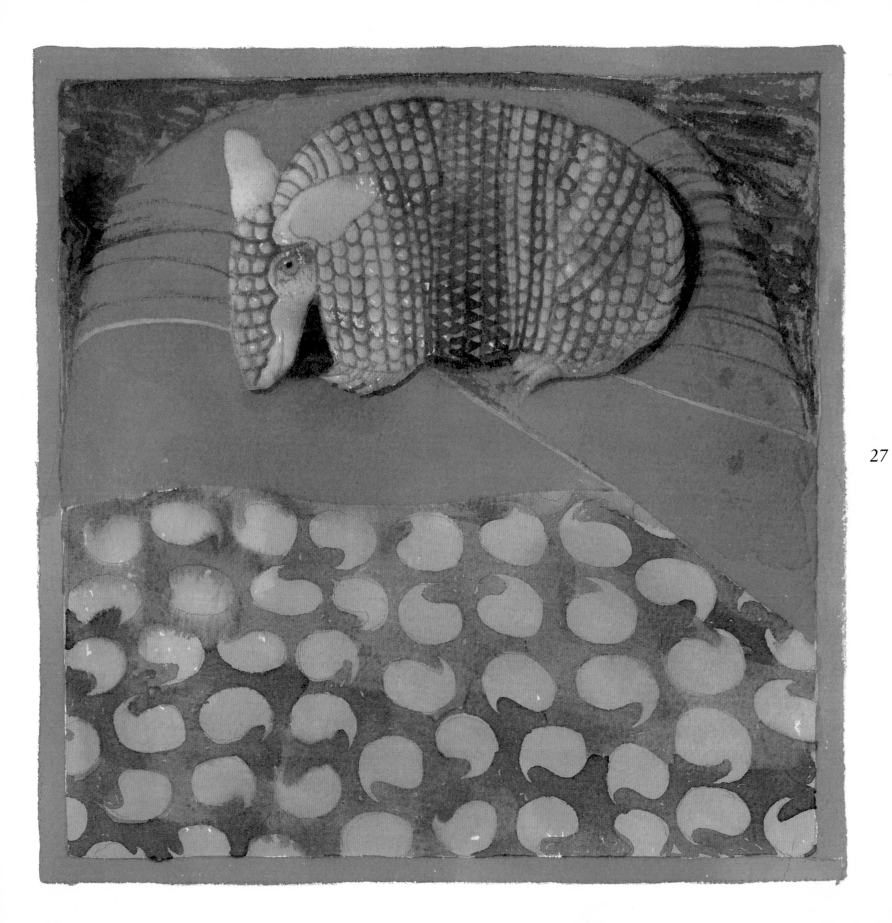

28

The Sloth

Up in a tree
The shaggy sloth
Is hanging by its claws.
It doesn't like to move at all.
It only likes to
p a u s e.

The Grasshopper

Green as a leaf.
Fast as a thief.
My olive eyes are
Oversized.
My two antennae
Grow and spread
Like tapered threads
Upon my head.
I hatch from eggs
With springs in my legs
And grind on grasses
As
   summer
       passes.

The Camel

The camel's altogether scary
With features haggard, harsh, and hairy.
It has a long and crooked neck
And giant feet to help it trek
Across the hot, dry desert sands
And over Asian prairie lands.
Upon its back a hairy hump
Arises like a beastly bump.
But do not fear the dreary camel.
It's not a monster —
It's a mammal.

The Caterpillar

The caterpillar's not a cat.
It's very small
And short and fat,
And with those beady little eyes
Will never win a beauty prize.
The caterpillar's brain is small —
It only knows to eat and crawl.
But for this creepy bug don't cry,
It soon will be a butterfly.

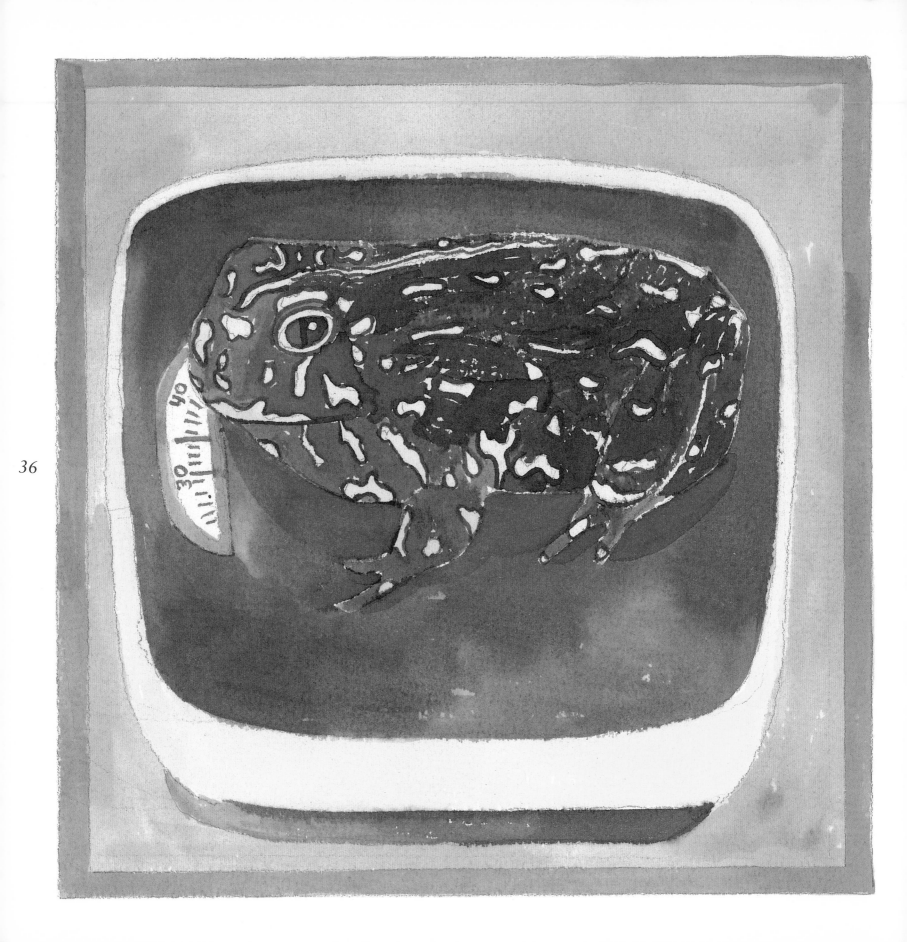

36

The Toad

The tubby toad's so squat and plump
That rarely does it even jump.
At night it feeds on worms and slugs,
Small spiders and assorted bugs,
Then hops into an earthy burrow
To dream of catching more tomorrow.

The Bat

The bat is batty as can be.
It sleeps all day in cave or tree,
And when the sun sets in the sky,
It rises from its rest to fly.
All night this mobile mammal mugs
A myriad of flying bugs.
And after its night out on the town,
The batty bat sleeps

Upside down.

38

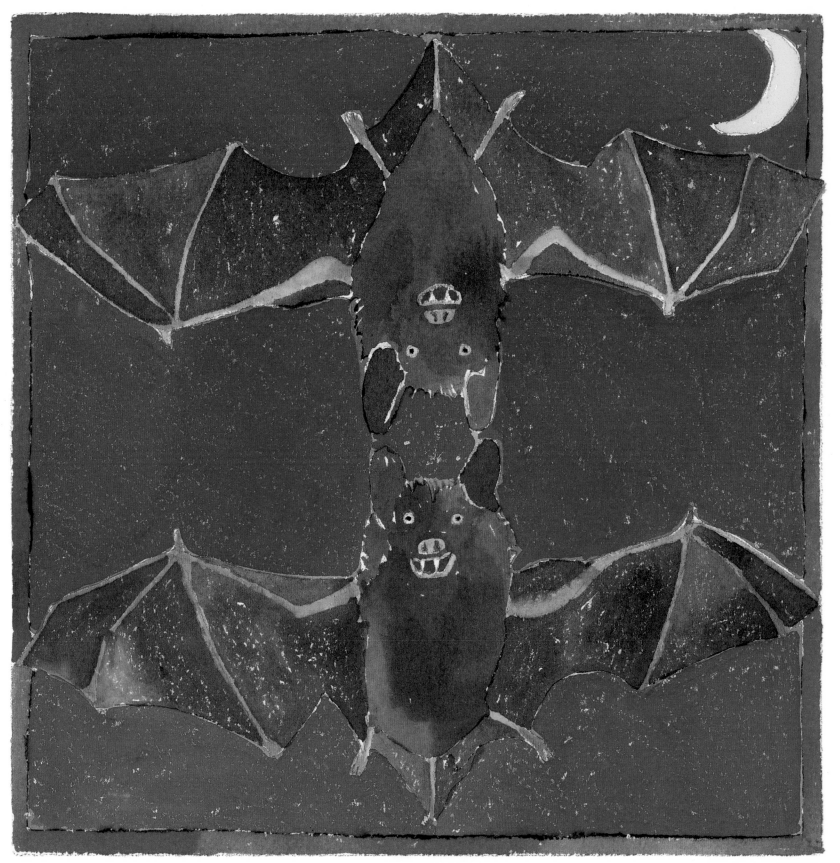

39

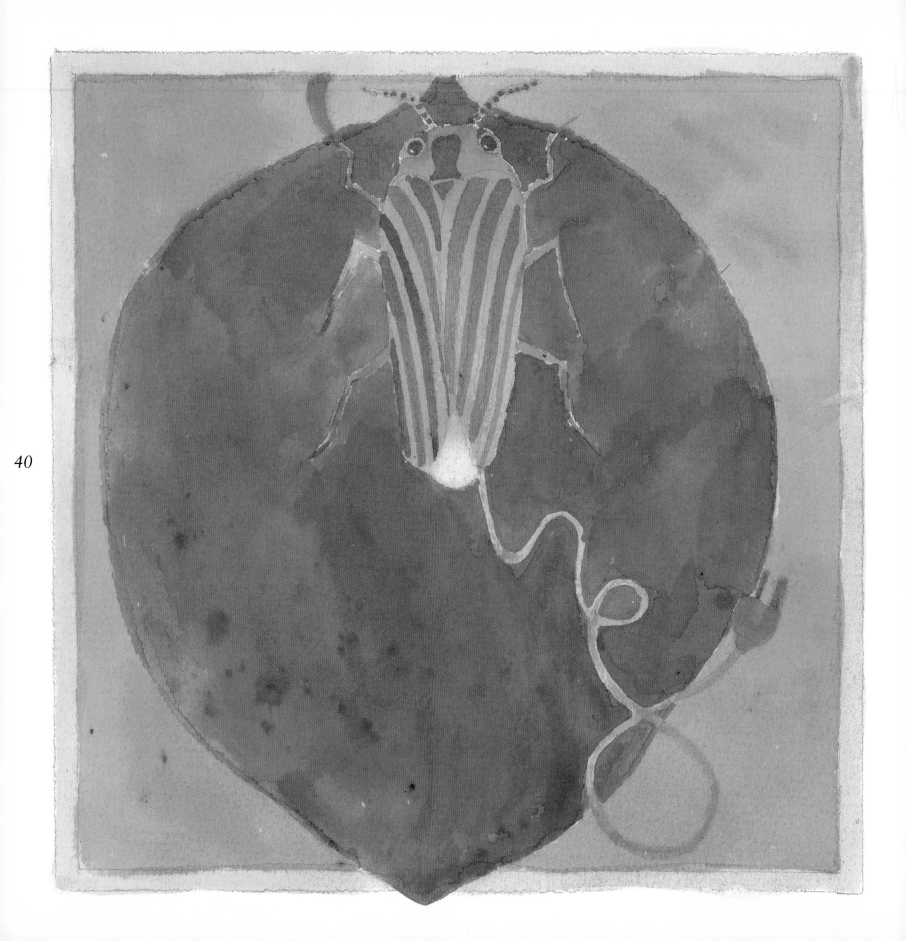

40

The Firefly

On August nights
The firefly lights
Blink
ON and OFF
Amongst the trees
But have no need
For batteries.

The Kangaroo

The kangaroo loves to leap.
Into the air it zooms,
While baby's fast asleep
Inside its kangaroom.

44

The Mole

The mole digs a hole with its toes
With help from its long pointed nose.
    By digging so thorough
    It makes a deep burrow
In which it can dreamily doze.

Its ears are not easily found
But perfect for picking up sound.
    Though virtually blind
    The mole doesn't mind—
There's not much to see underground.

45

The Kiwi

Wings so small.
No tail at all.
Very rare.
Feathers like hair.
Quiet and shy.
Cannot fly.
They call you a bird,
But I don't know why.

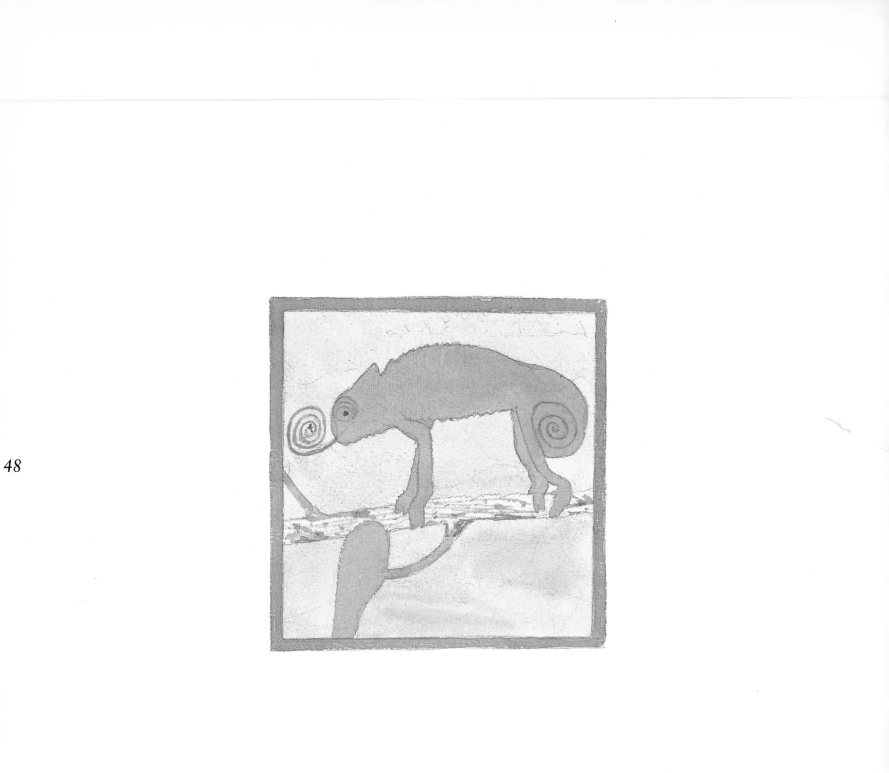

10/95 Beast Wishes! Doug Florian

poems and paintings by

Douglas Florian